Watson!

CHARLIE PIECHART
and the case of the
Missing Dog

To Charlie's angels, Lori, Jill, and Dana. Charlie would not be
if it were not for your expertise and care. Thank you.

—E.C.

To all my dog-loving family and friends—
Stan, Marilyn, Kristin, Mike, Paul, Donna, Shannon, Lauren,
John, Cathy, Susan, Cindy, Jan, Michaela, Trenayce, Gordon,
Joe, Jim, and Sharon: Please help us find Watson!

—M.S.

Charlie Piechart and the Case of the Missing Dog
Text copyright © 2018 by Marilyn Sadler and Eric Comstock
Illustrations copyright © 2018 by Eric Comstock
All rights reserved. Manufactured in China.
No part of this book may be used or reproduced in any manner whatsoever without written permission except in the case of
brief quotations embodied in critical articles and reviews. For information address HarperCollins Children's Books, a division of
HarperCollins Publishers, 195 Broadway, New York, NY 10007.
www.harpercollinschildrens.com

Library of Congress Control Number: 2017943579
ISBN 978-0-06-237058-7

The artist used pencil, paper, Adobe Illustrator, and Adobe Photoshop to create the digital illustrations for this book.
Typography by Eric Comstock and Dana Fritts
18 19 20 21 22 SCP 10 9 8 7 6 5 4 3 2 1

First Edition

CHARLIE PIECHART

and the case of the
Missing Dog

written by
ERIC COMSTOCK & MARILYN SADLER
illustrated by ERIC COMSTOCK

HARPER
An Imprint of HarperCollins Publishers

a CHARLIE PIECHART mystery

"Charlie, have you seen Watson?" asked Mrs. Piechart. "I can't find that dog anywhere."

Watson had a **4:15 p.m.** appointment at Dirty Dog Groomers for a shampoo and haircut. It was already **3:30 p.m.** They needed to find him soon!

They had ½ **an hour** to find Watson. That's **30 minutes.**

I'm on the case!

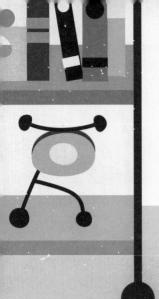

Lewis's Watch ↘

I can help, too.

3:30 P.M.

DIGI-WATCH

This is what 3:30 p.m. looks like on a digital watch.

Charlie asked everyone in the family where and at what time they had last seen Watson, and he kept track in his notebook.

9:30 a.m. 10:30 a.m.

Charlie and Watson went skateboarding together after lunch at **12:30 p.m.**

12:30 p.m.   1:30 p.m.   2:30 p.m.   3:30 p.m.

3 HOURS

12:30 p.m.

That was 3 hours ago.

Kate and Alice saw Watson at **1:15 p.m.** when they tried to paint his nails, but Watson ran away before his polish was dry.

Watson Sightings

Dad   8:00 a.m.
Backyard

Mom   9:30 a.m.
kitchen

Me   12:30 p.m.
Skatepark

Kate & Alice   1:15 p.m.
Bedroom

Lewis and Charlie looked for a clue. Charlie spotted some Puppy Loves Pink nail polish on the floor.

The boys followed the trail of nail polish into the kitchen and up onto the counter to the cookie jar . . .

. . . which was broken! And there on the floor was a trail of cookie crumbs leading . . .

... to Charlie's room!

The trail ended under Charlie's bed. The floor
was still warm, but there was no Watson!

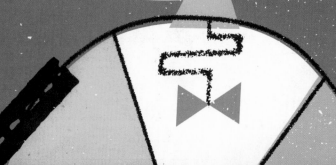

When Charlie and Lewis ran out to the backyard, they heard noise coming from Watson's doghouse.

But Watson wasn't there.

A trail of cards led them to the front yard,
where Charlie's dad was raking leaves.

LE

I KNOW H

WATSO

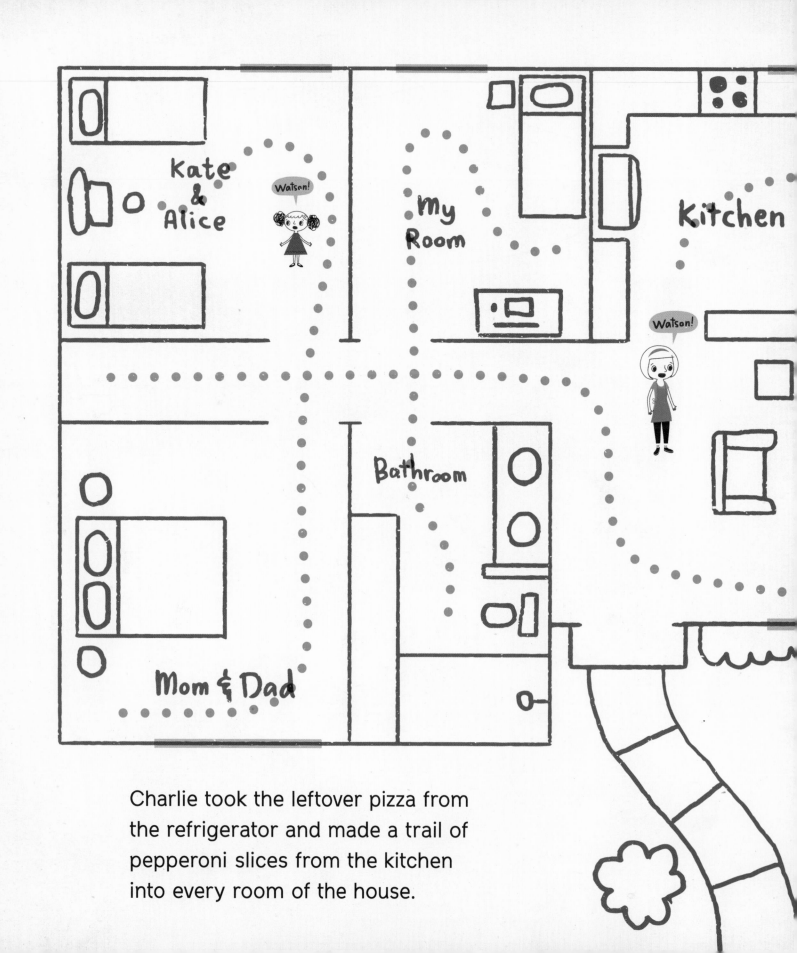

Charlie took the leftover pizza from the refrigerator and made a trail of pepperoni slices from the kitchen into every room of the house.

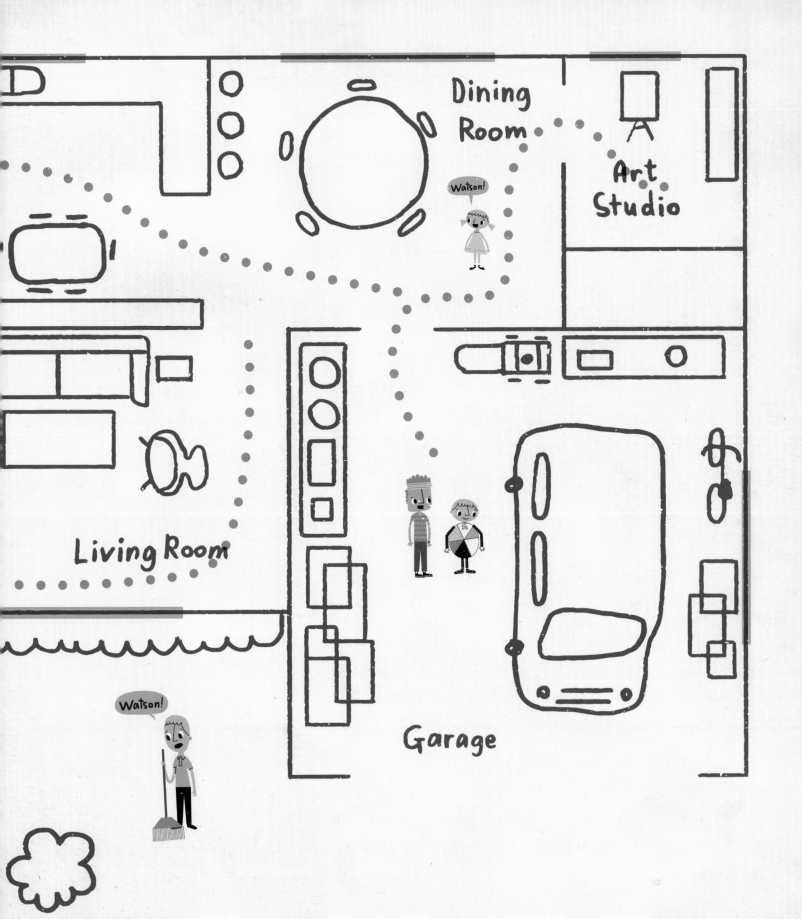

They ran out of pepperoni in the garage.

It was already **4:00 p.m.** They had **15 minutes** to get Watson to his **4:15 p.m.** Dirty Dog appointment on time!

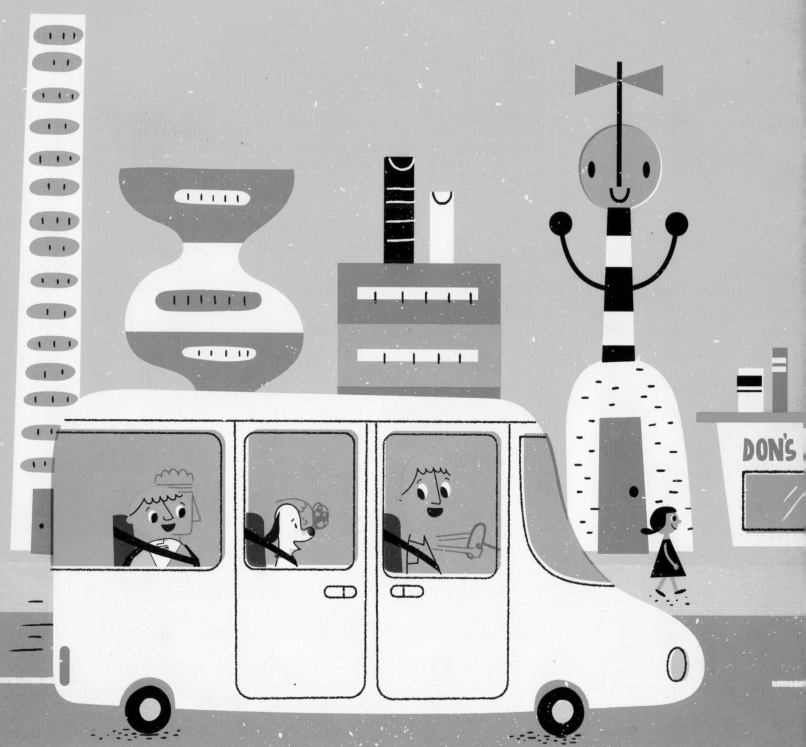

Watson got his scrub-a-dub-dub as the Piecharts looked on. At last, he would be clean again!

THERE ARE 60 MINUTES IN AN HOUR

5 MINUTES

The LITTLE HAND tells you the hour. It's 3:00!

The BIG HAND tells you the minute.

1 2 3 4 5 6 7 8 9 10 11 12